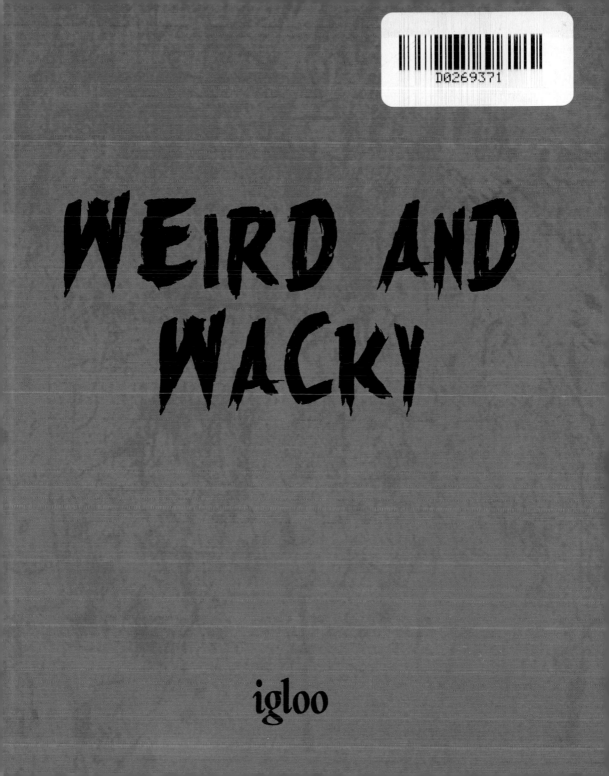

WEIRD AND WACKY

igloo

The Weird Wishes

Karl and Andy stared at the wooden box they had just discovered in Andy's back yard. It was about the size of a shoebox and covered in strange carvings. "It looks weird," said Andy, "Don't open it."

Karl ignored his friend and tried to pry the lid off. With a loud crack, the lid flipped open. There was a musty waft of air, then a scaly creature flew out and hovered next to them. The creature looked like a lizard, with bright eyes, purple scales, a yellow belly and a long, swishing tail. It had hands like a monkey's paws, and a big, grinning mouth.

"What is it?" gasped Andy.
To their surprise, the creature answered. "I'm a genie," it said.
"You don't look like a genie," said Karl. "Genies come out of lamps. They wear earrings and pointy shoes."

The creature hissed at the boys. "I am not a genie of fairytales," it said. "You have three wishes. What's your first one?"

Before Andy had a chance to speak, Karl blurted out a wish.
"I wish we looked like really cool monsters." he said.
"Your wish is my command!" said the genie.

The Weird Wishes

The genie swished its tail and the boys began to shiver and change.
Karl had clawed feet, green hair, orange skin and horns coming out of his
forehead. Andy was covered in fur and had big ears and fangs. The friends
looked at each other in amazement.

When Andy's little sister saw her brother and his friend, she screamed and
ran upstairs. "Monsters!" she cried. Andy and Karl went out into the street to
see their friends, but their friends yelled in fright.
"Help!" they shrieked. "We're being attacked!"

Everyone on the street stopped and stared at the monster boys. Some people
laughed and others screamed. "Get them!" someone cried. "They're monsters!"

The Weird Wishes

"Run!" shouted Andy, and they fled down the street. They heard police sirens and found that they were heading straight towards a police car. It screeched to a halt just as they raced down a side street.

The genie was cackling behind the escaping boys. Suddenly, the alleyway turned into a dead end. The policeman chased after them, followed by a big crowd of angry-looking people. "This is horrible," said Karl, "I wish there was a way to fight back!"

"Your wish is my command!" said the genie.

The Weird Wishes

Suddenly, Karl and Andy felt themselves growing. They started to rise above the people, until they were giant-sized. Karl leaned down towards the crowd and roared, as loud as he could. The people scattered in fear.
"That's more like it!" Karl said.
"I'll race you to the top of that tower block over there!" said Andy.

The monster friends easily climbed to the top of the tower block, where they could look out over all of the city. They heard a buzzing sound in the distance. It was a swarm of police helicopters, coming to chase them.

Andy tried to swat them as they flew past, but he leaned too far over the edge and lost his balance. "Help!" he cried, as he toppled off the edge of the building.

The Weird Wishes

Karl remembered that he still had a wish. "I wish Andy could fly," he said to the genie. There was a moment of silence and then Andy reappeared, flapping huge bat-wings. The helicopters flew away in fright.

Andy landed and sat next to Karl. "This isn't fun at all," he said. "Everyone hates us and we've used up all of our wishes."

The genie gave a sinister laugh. "I like seeing everyone make a mess of their wishes. You've used them up and now you will stay looking like monsters." "Wait," said Andy, "Genie, you granted Karl his three wishes, but what about my three?"

The genie looked annoyed. "Oh, I suppose you can have three, too," he grunted.

"Okay," said Andy, "first, I wish we looked like ourselves again."
Karl and Andy shivered, and found that they were back to their normal size and shape. "Now I wish we were all back in the garden," said Andy. The genie lashed its tail and a fierce wind blew up. It picked them up and whirled them back to Andy's back yard.

"And finally," said Andy, "I wish that you, genie, would return to your box and not come out."

"Nooo!" cried the genie, but it had no choice. With a whoosh, it flitted back into the box. The lid slammed shut, sealing the genie inside.

"Phew," said Karl, "thanks for using your wishes to save us, Andy."

Andy and Karl buried the box deep in the yard, where nobody would ever find it. Andy switched the portable radio on. "Breaking news," said the announcer, "mystery monsters have run amok in the city!"

"Do you think anyone would believe us if we said those monsters were us?" Karl asked Andy. "We could be famous!"

"You wish!" Andy said, laughing.

The Lethal Laboratory

Jules and Ruby stood outside the creepy mansion, with their suitcases. They weren't too keen on the idea of spending a weekend with their eccentric, Great Uncle Bertram. However, Mum had insisted that it was about time their reclusive relative came out of his shell, so here they were.

Great Uncle Bertram appeared in the doorway with a sullen, unwelcoming grin on his face. He wore a white lab coat and had the thickest, roundest glasses they'd ever seen. His hair hung like limp noodles around his head and his tight grin made him look quite sinister.

"I suppose you had better come in," he mumbled. "I don't know why people can't just leave me alone to get on with my work."

Great Uncle Bertram continued to mutter under his breath as he showed Jules and Ruby around the dilapidated house. They had never seen anywhere so big, or so empty. Every room was bare and it was freezing cold. In the middle of the massive hall, there was a big trapdoor.

"What's down there?" asked Ruby.
"Never you mind," snapped Great Uncle Bertram, "you must never go down there, that's my laboratory. Now off to bed with you, I have work to do."

That night, after a supper of stale bread and cold baked beans, Jules and Ruby went to bed. Huge moths flapped in the moonlight and spiders scuttled up the walls. Downstairs, strange groans came from Uncle Bertram's laboratory.

The next morning, Jules and Ruby asked Great Uncle Bertram about the strange noises in the night. Their great uncle turned purple with rage. "Don't ask me questions and keep your noses out of my laboratory," he warned.

"Something is under that trapdoor in the hall," said Ruby when their great uncle went down into his laboratory, "and whatever it is, it wants to get out. I think we should go down there tonight and find out what's going on."

The Lethal Laboratory

That night, when they were sure Great Uncle Bertram was asleep, Jules and Ruby crept downstairs and through the trapdoor. Bottles of dangerous-looking chemicals bubbled and smoked on a large table. A huge electricity generator sparked and fizzed in one corner.

In the centre of the room, a motionless creature was chained to a large slab. It looked a bit like an ape and a bit like a man, but with large, furred ears like a wolf and big, pointed horns like a stag. "I think it's dead," said Jules. He poked the creature and the monster sat up, suddenly, with a deep grunt.

Jules and Ruby screamed as the monster twisted and struggled. It groaned and yanked at the chains until, finally, they snapped.

The Lethal Laboratory

The creature jumped off the slab and came towards Jules and Ruby, who cowered in a corner. The grunting noises got louder. Suddenly, Jules realized that the monster wasn't trying to harm them, it was trying to say something to them. Its cries sounded almost like speech.

"Help me," said the beast, in a strange, gurgling voice. It held out its hands. "I was captured in the forest. Please set me free."

Ruby and Jules looked at each other. The poor creature looked so sad. Ruby put her hand out and the creature took it in its huge paw.

Cautiously, the children crept up the steps and opened the trapdoor. It made a horrible creak that seemed to echo around the house.

Ruby tried to open the locked front door. The creature raised its huge paws to smash it, but Ruby stopped him. "Sssh, you'll wake Great Uncle Bertram," she hissed.

Jules went to check that Great Uncle Bertram was still asleep. He opened his bedroom door to see an empty bed. Jules quickly rushed back down the stairs. "We have to get back to the lab, quickly," he gasped.

As Ruby and the creature reached the laboratory, a steel cage fell down around them, with a gigantic crash. "So, you have found my creature," said Great Uncle Bertram with a malicious laugh. "Do not try to escape, the bars of the cage are electrified."

Great Uncle Bertram explained how he had captured the beast in the forest. "I knew its discovery would make me the most famous scientist in the world," he said with a sly, greedy smile.

Ruby could see that Jules was creeping slowly down the stairs behind Great Uncle Bertram. Suddenly, Jules leaped forward and gave his great uncle such a shove he fell against the electrified bars of the cage.

Jules rushed over and pulled the lever so that the bars of the cage lifted. Ruby and the creature stumbled out and followed Jules back up the steps and into the hallway.

Once in the hall, the beast ran to the door and with one mighty blow, he smashed it down and fled into the forest. "Thank you, friends," he cried as he disappeared into the dark forest. Ruby and Jules turned to see two bright car headlights coming up the drive towards them.

"It's Mum and Dad!" cried Ruby, rushing into the arms of her father. "We just thought we would come and see how you are doing," said Mum. "Great Uncle Bertram can be a bit unpredictable, sometimes."

Ruby and Jules looked at each other. Then they looked at the scowling figure of Great Uncle Bertram, who had recovered and staggered outside. "Yes, we know," they said.

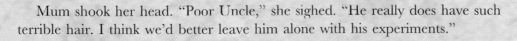

Mum shook her head. "Poor Uncle," she sighed. "He really does have such terrible hair. I think we'd better leave him alone with his experiments."

"What a good idea!" said Ruby and Jules, as they waved goodbye to Great Uncle Bertram and the lethal laboratory, forever.

The Stone Horseman

Lee and Ged had almost reached the cave. They were on an adventure holiday with their friends, camping in the middle of a vast rainforest. Everyone else had got tired and gone back to camp, but Lee and Ged wanted more excitement.

The entrance to the cave was matted with cobwebs. "It looks like nobody's been here for a very long time," said Lee. The boys broke through the webs and stepped into a wide, airy cave. A shaft of light shone on to a massive statue of a helmeted man, carrying a huge sword and riding a rearing horse.
The statue was made of dark marble, with dark red lines running through it that almost looked like veins.

"It's a bit creepy," said Lee, but Ged interrupted him.
"Look at this!" he cried. On another stone plinth, near the statue, was an enormous, glittering, blood-red, jewel. "This will make a great souvenir," said Ged, grabbing the jewel. Suddenly, there was a huge crashing sound and a great cloud of dust whirled round the cave. When it cleared, Lee and Ged saw that the Stone Horseman had gone too.

The boys were spooked and stood in silence. Cold shivers ran down their spines. "I don't like it here," stammered Lee.
"Me, neither," said Ged, "I think we should leave." The two boys scrambled out into the sunlight and ran back towards the camp. They ran so fast, they didn't notice the giant hoofprints leading off into the forest.

Back at the camp, the boys showed the jewel to their friend, George. "You shouldn't have taken this," he warned, "there are all sorts of legends about this forest." But Lee and Ged were far too frightened to go back to the cave.

That night, just as they were going to sleep, the boys heard a noise outside their tent. It was a low, deep, thundering sound, like giant hooves. Suddenly, the jewel began to glow in the darkness. Ged and Lee were terrified. They lay awake all night, waiting for the Stone Horseman to ride over them, but after some time, the sounds gradually faded into silence.

The next morning, Lee found hoofprints all around the tent. They were far bigger than any horse he'd ever seen. "It wants the jewel back," said Lee.

Ged knew that what he said was true.

The Stone Horseman

That day's activity was a rafting trip down the river. The boys were so busy trying to stay in the boat, they almost forgot about the Stone Horseman.
That was until Ged saw a large, shadowy figure, lurking in a clump of trees along the riverbank. Ged pulled Lee's arm to get his attention, but when they looked round, the figure had gone.

That evening, Lee and Ged were both nervous. George came to see them and they all kept looking out for dark shapes in the trees around the camp.

The Stone Horseman

"I don't like this," said Lee, "we should never have taken that jewel."
As he spoke, the sound of thundering hooves filled the air. The trees shook and the Stone Horseman burst through.

George and Ged dived to the floor, as the Stone Horseman leaped right over them, landing with a crashing sound. "This way!" yelled Lee, dashing into the bushes.

In the near distance, lights came on and they could hear shouting as the camp woke up. George dived into a tent. Ged followed Lee, as he scrambled up a ledge to look down on the camp. Below, the Stone Horseman charged around and raised its sword, threateningly.

Ged took the glowing jewel out of his pocket. "This is what it wants," he said. Suddenly, the Stone Horseman noticed the jewel. He galloped straight up the ledge towards the boys. "Run!" cried Ged, "we've got to get this jewel back to the cave."

Lee and Ged clambered to the very top of the rocky incline and scrambled down the other side, into the forest. Behind them, the sound of hooves clattering on rock grew louder. Ged took the jewel out of his pocket. It glowed and seemed to be pulling him in a particular direction. "This must be the way back to the cave," he said. "Come on, let's go."

The boys sprinted through the sweltering forest, guided by the stone. The sounds of tree branches tearing and crashing behind them made them run even faster.

After what seemed like ages, the cave came into sight. The boys were exhausted, but they could hear the thundering of hooves right behind them. The trees were shaking and, in an instant, the Stone Horseman had burst through the leaves and was galloping at full speed, to get his revenge.

Ged and Lee hurtled into the cave, tripping and stumbling towards the plinth. The whole cave shook as the Stone Horseman entered. At that moment, Ged placed the jewel back on its plinth.